Clifford THE BIG RED DOG®

The Costume Contest

by Mariah Balaban

Illustrated by Steve Haefele

Based on the Scholastic book series
"Clifford The Big Red Dog"
by Norman Bridwell

12 11 10 9 8 7 6   12/0

Printed in the U.S.A.   40
First printing, September 2008

SCHOLASTIC INC.

New York   Toronto   London   Auckland   Sydney
Mexico City   New Delhi   Hong Kong   Buenos Aires

It was the day before Halloween.

Cleo and T-Bone were excited.

"I can't wait to go trick-or-treating," said Cleo.

"I can't wait to dress up," said T-Bone.

Clifford didn't say anything.

He didn't have a Halloween costume.

"I'll help you find a Halloween costume,"
Emily Elizabeth said to Clifford.

Emily Elizabeth took Clifford to the store.

At the store, Clifford tried on a hat

and glasses.

They were too small.

Next Clifford tried on bunny ears and bunny tail.

They were too silly.

"You don't need a costume, Clifford," said Emily Elizabeth.

"You're perfect just the way you are!"

Clifford didn't think so. He wanted a costume.

The next night was Halloween.

Everyone met in the village center to go
trick-or-treating.

They showed off their colorful costumes.

Emily Elizabeth was a pirate.

Cleo was a witch.

T-Bone was a superhero.

Mac was a lion.

Clifford was still Clifford.

He did not have a costume, so he was hiding.

"Where's Clifford?" Cleo asked.

"If he does not come soon, he will miss all the fun," said T-Bone.

Emily Elizabeth and her friends stopped at each house in the village.

"Trick or treat!" called Emily Elizabeth.

Mac did a trick.

Everyone got a treat.

"It's too bad that Clifford is missing the treats," said T-Bone.

After trick-or-treating, they went to Emily Elizabeth's house to carve pumpkins.

Emily Elizabeth carved a great big one.

"This pumpkin is for Clifford," she said.

This pumpkin will make a perfect hiding place!
Clifford thought.

Clifford crawled into the giant jack-o'-lantern.

"Now I can watch the party!" he said.

Clifford peered out of the two big eyes.

Soon Clifford grew tired.

"This pumpkin is too small for me,"
Clifford said.

Then he had an idea.

He carefully dug five holes in the pumpkin.

The holes were just big enough for
Clifford's legs and his tail.
Now he could stretch out.
He could even walk around.
That was much better!

Meanwhile, Emily Elizabeth and
her friends were bobbing for apples.
"It's time for the costume contest.
Let's go!" said Emily Elizabeth.

They all went out onto the lawn.

They stood in a line for the costume contest.

Mr. and Mrs. Howard were the judges.

"Look, it's Clifford!" called Emily Elizabeth.
"I knew that you would find a costume," she
said to Clifford.

Clifford looked at himself in the window.

He did not see a Big Red Dog.

He saw a big orange pumpkin instead.

He barked happily.

He had a costume after all!

Clifford was just in time for the contest.

Emily Elizabeth's costume was the most adventurous.

Charley's costume was the scariest.

Clifford's costume was the biggest.

"Clifford, you win first prize!" said

Mr. Howard.

Clifford was very proud and very happy.

After the costume contest, Clifford's friends
shared their Halloween treats with him.
That made him even happier!

Do You Remember?

Circle the right answer.

1. What costume did Clifford try on first?
   - a. A hat and glasses
   - b. A big pumpkin
   - c. Bunny ears and a bunny tail

2. Why was Clifford hiding?
   - a. He did not like Halloween.
   - b. He wanted a costume.
   - c. He felt sick.

Which happened first?

Which happened next?

Which happened last?

Write a 1, 2, or 3 in the space after each sentence.

Clifford hides inside a jack-o'-lantern. _____

Emily Elizabeth takes Clifford to the store. _____

Clifford's friends share their Halloween treats with him. ____

Will Clifford ever find a costume?

**You can read this funny
story by yourself!**

RL 1.5
AGES 5–8

ISBN-13: 978-0-545-09921-9
ISBN-10: 0-545-09921-8

EAN

9 780545 099219

SCHOLASTIC

scholastic.com/clifford

Clifford THE BIG RED DOG®

BIG RED READER™

THE COSTUME CONTEST

SCHOLASTIC